NORMAN BRIDWELL

Clifford's
MANNERS

Sh-h-h!

Dedicated to Robbie and Alex

Library of Congress Cataloging-in-Publication Data

Bridwell, Norman.
Clifford's manners / Norman Bridwell.
p.   cm.
Summary: Everyone loves Clifford, the big red dog, because Emily
Elizabeth has taught him such beautiful manners.
ISBN 0-590-48697-7
[1. Etiquette — Fiction. 2. Dogs — Fiction.] I. Title.
PZ7.B7633Cng   1994
[E] — dc20   94-4004
CIP
AC

12 11 10 9 8 7 6 5 4 3 2 1   11   4 5 6 7 8 9/9
Printed in the U.S.A.   24

NORMAN BRIDWELL
Clifford's
MANNERS

WELCOME

SCHOLASTIC INC.
New York

SCHOLASTIC
HARDCOVER

I'm Emily Elizabeth,
and this is Clifford.

Everyone loves Clifford
because he has good manners.
I taught him myself.

Clifford says "please" when he asks for something.

Say please.

Say thank
you.

He says "thank you" when he gets something.

And he writes a thank-you note
when someone gives him a present.

Wait your turn.

Clifford loves to go to the movies.
He waits his turn in line.

If Clifford has a snack,
he puts the empty bag into the litter basket.
Clifford hates litterbugs.

Don't litter.

Say excuse
me.

Clifford says "excuse me" when he needs
to pass in front of people.

He never talks during the show.
Talking disturbs others.

Do not talk
during a show.

Sh-h-h!

Use your handkerchief.

KERTY-SHOO

When Clifford has to sneeze,
he uses a handkerchief or tissue.
It's a good thing he does.

Clifford has many friends.
He shares his toys with them.

Share.

Put your toys away.

Clifford puts his toys away when he is through.
His friends help. They have good manners, too.

Clifford is a terrific tennis player.
He obeys all the rules of the game.

**Follow the
rules.**

Talk—
don't hit.

Sometimes players disagree.
When Clifford is angry, he does not hit.
He just says what he feels.

Clifford is a good sport.
He smiles when he loses.
And he does not boast when he wins.

CLIFFORD | 4 | 4 | 5
EMILY | 6 | 6 | 7

Be a good
sport.

Call ahead.

Clifford loves to go visiting.
When he visits his sister in the country,
he always calls ahead.

Clifford always arrives on time.

Don't be late.

**Knock before
you walk in.**

He knocks on the door before he enters.

He wipes his feet first.

Wipe your
feet.

Clifford kisses his sister.
He shakes hands with her friend.

Shake hands.

Wash up
before
you eat.

Clifford's sister has dinner ready.
Clifford washes his hands before he eats.

Clifford chews his food with his mouth closed.
He never talks with his mouth full.

**Don't talk
with your
mouth full.**

Clifford helps with the clean-up.

Help clean up.

Say
good-bye.

Then he says "thank you" and "good-bye"
to his sister and to her friend.

Everyone loves Clifford's manners.
That's why everyone loves Clifford!

Have good
manners.